words by
JORDAN MAYER

LEROY
the Raccoon

This book is dedicated to my friend Dorothy Ryan,
who taught me to eat dessert first!
JORDAN MAYER

This book is dedicated to my nephews, Rhodes and Gunnar.
ROBYN LEAVENS

Tellwell Talent
www.tellwell.ca

JORDAN MAYER
Leroy the Raccoon
Text copyright © 2022 by Jordan Mayer
Illustrations copyright © 2022 by Robyn Leavens
First Edition

Paperback ISBN: 978-0-2288-7836-0

Book Design | Robyn Leavens
Typeset in Hecho A Mano
Publishing Support | TellWell Publishing

LEROY
the Raccoon

words by
JORDAN MAYER

pictures by
ROBYN LEAVENS

MEET LEROY

Meet Leroy! He's cute, kind and loveable, but he might mishear you from time to time. Don't let that bother you though, he means well ... truly!

Join Leroy as he shares different lessons that he's learned on his adventures. He hopes you'll quickly become friends and learn that raccoons aren't so bad after all!

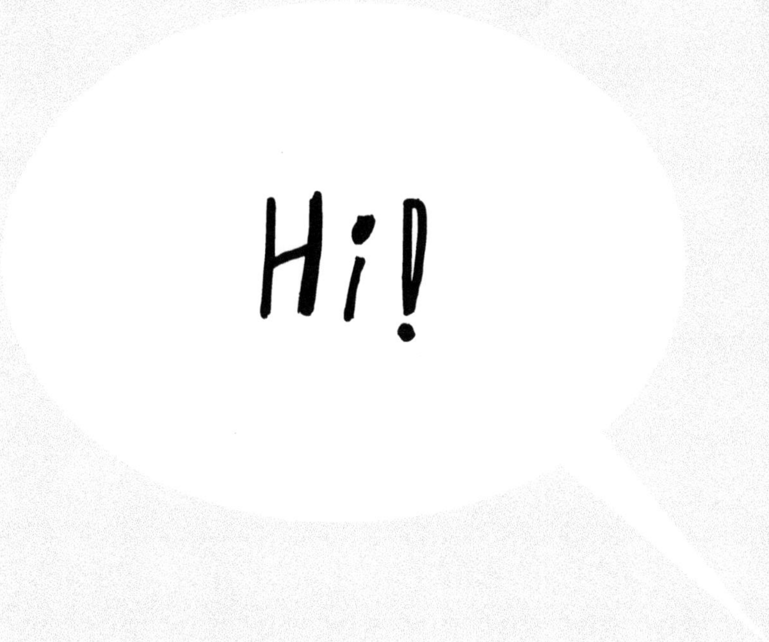
Hi!

Did you know
that my
favourite game
to play is hide
and seek?

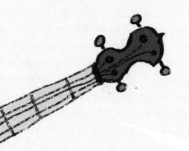

We didn't know each other a few minutes ago and now I'm proud to call you my friend.

Author's Note

Early one morning, I took my dog Pippin outside for a quick walk. I took a few steps and there, right in front of us stood a large, scary looking raccoon! It's eyes were red and when I tried to scare it away, the raccoon didn't move a muscle. Yikes! As I moved back towards the door, I saw another raccoon sitting on a fence just above my head. I quickly rushed inside and shut the door behind me. Breathing heavily I thought: Those are the meanest, grossest animals I have ever seen. I never want to see a raccoon ever again!

A few days later, I was thinking about my encounter with those garbage eating bandits. I wondered if they were really so bad after all or if I simply had a bad first impression. That made me think about other people I've met in my life. At first, they may have seemed mean or selfish, however, once I got to know them, they weren't so bad after all. In fact, many of them have become my friends.

I thought it would be fun to write a series about a raccoon named Leroy. It's my hope that you take some time to get to know him and realize that you may have more in common with him than you might realize!

About the Author

Jordan is a husband, father of two and educator in British Columbia, Canada. He is passionate about helping children fall in love with the process of learning and showing them that the world is a wonder-full place! In his spare time, Jordan enjoys playing basketball, learning new recipes and going on walks with his family.

About the Illustrator

Robyn Leavens loves to illustrate children's books and lives in New Westminster, British Columbia, with her lovely husband, Sheldon, and two fluffy cats, Taika and Tumnus. She loves to draw, laugh, walk about in forests and eat sushi. You can see more of her illustrations at robynleavens.com.

CPSIA information can be obtained
at www.ICGtesting.com
Printed in the USA
BVHW091920221022
650024BV00005B/122